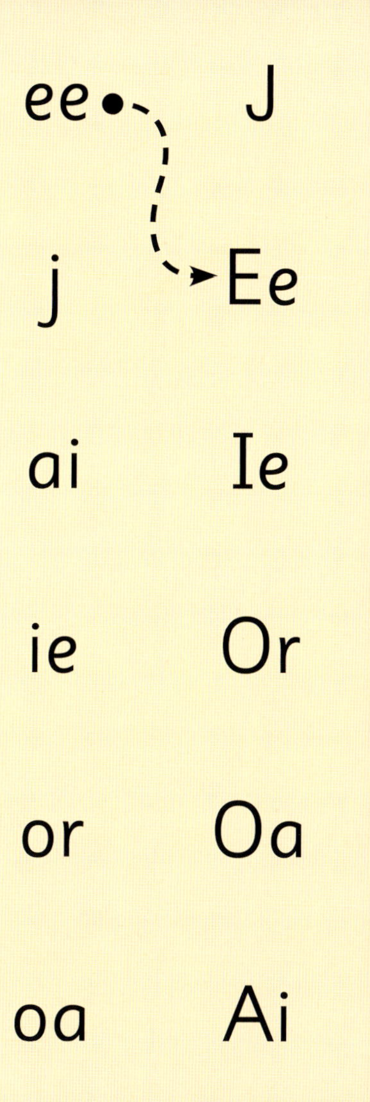

Gail, Jill, and Dad set off for Red Jack's Fort.

Dad's jeep creeps up a steep hill.

Red Jack's Fort has a deep moat.

Gail jumps, but Jill is afraid.

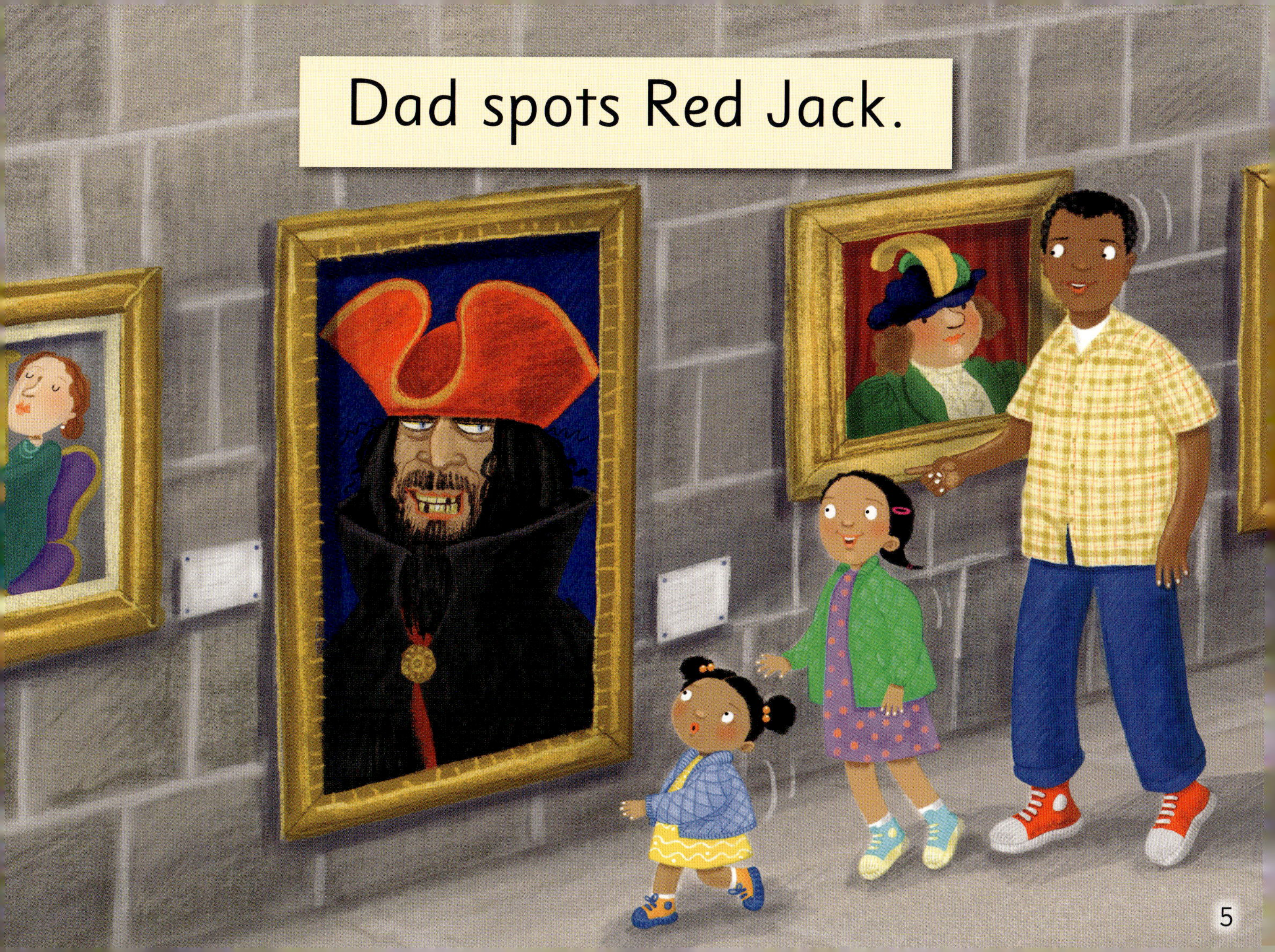

Dad spots Red Jack.

At ten, Dad stops for coffee.

Gail has milk, toast, and jam.

Jill has a pie.

A gull flies in for Gail's crusts!

Jill sees Red Jack's hat and cloak.

Gail spies Red Jack’s boat.

Beep, beep!